DICK KING-

Back-to-Front
Benjy

Illustrated by Judy Brown

PUFFIN BOOKS

PUFFIN BOOKS

Published by the Penguin Group
Penguin Books Ltd, 27 Wrights Lane, London W8 5TZ, England
Penguin Putnam Inc., 375 Hudson Street, New York, New York 10014, USA
Penguin Books Australia Ltd, Ringwood, Victoria, Australia
Penguin Books Canada Ltd, 10 Alcorn Avenue, Toronto, Ontario, Canada M4V 3B2
Penguin Books India (P) Ltd, 11 Community Centre, Panchsheel Park,
New Delhi – 110 017, India
Penguin Books (NZ) Ltd, Cnr Rosedale and Airborne Roads, Albany,
Auckland, New Zealand
Penguin Books (South Africa) (Pty) Ltd, 5 Watkins Street, Denver Ext 4,
Johannesburg 2094, South Africa

On the World Wide Web at: www.penguin.com

Penguin Books Ltd, Registered Offices: Harmondsworth, Middlesex, England

First published 2001
1

Set in Baskerville MT

Made and printed in England by Clays Ltd, St Ives plc

British Library Cataloguing in Publication Data
A CIP catalogue record for this book is available from the British Library

ISBN 0–141–31077–4

Back-to-Front Benjy

Dick King-Smith served in the Grenadier Guards during the Second World War, and afterwards spent twenty years as a farmer in Gloucestershire, the county of his birth. Many of his stories are inspired by his farming experiences. Later he taught at a village primary school. His first book, *The Fox Busters*, was published in 1978. Since then he has written a great number of children's books, including *The Sheep-Pig* (winner of the *Guardian* Award and filmed as *Babe*), *Harry's Mad*, *Noah's Brother*, *The Hodgeheg*, *Martin's Mice*, *Ace*, *The Cuckoo Child* and *Harriet's Hare* (winner of the Children's Book Award in 1995). At the British Book Awards in 1992 he was voted Children's Author of the Year. He has three children, twelve grandchildren and two great-grandchildren, and lives in a seventeenth-century cottage a short crow's-flight from the house where he was born.

Contents

Back-to-Front Benjy

It was funny, but the very first time that Maggie Mills met Bill Butterworth, they were both travelling backwards. The train was of course travelling forwards, and a very crowded train it was, so that there were only two empty seats left in that compartment. Two seats side by side, with their backs to the engine.

No sooner had Maggie sat down in the one by the window than a voice said, 'Excuse me, is this other seat taken?' Maggie said 'No' and a man sat down beside her.

'Train's crowded this morning, isn't it?' he said.

'Yes,' replied Maggie.

Hope he's not going to be a chatterer, she thought, and she shot a sideways glance at him. He was smiling. It was rather a nice smile, she thought.

'Don't worry,' said the man. 'I'm not a chatterer.' Which of course made Maggie feel awkward, so that

she smiled back at him. It was rather
a nice smile, he thought.

'I always like to ride with my back
to the engine,' she said.

'Me too,' said the man, and then
they began to talk as they travelled
backwards at high speed, and before

long he told her his name and she told him hers, and it somehow seemed quite natural that they should be going to the same destination.

'I hope perhaps we may meet again,' said Bill Butterworth as they parted outside the railway station. 'I always come up on the eight twenty-three.'

'Me too,' said Maggie.

'Well then,' said Bill, 'I'll say goodbye for now.' And he put out a hand and Maggie shook it.

Now I'm going to press the fast-forward button and tell you that Maggie and Bill did meet again many times on the 8.23 (always travelling backwards, of course).

They chattered away to each other nineteen to the dozen and found themselves becoming fond of one another. One day Bill Butterworth proposed to Maggie Mills – on the train – and she accepted and they were married and about a year later Maggie Butterworth had a baby boy.

Benjamin Butterworth appeared to be an absolutely normal baby. He put on weight, he slept well, and when he was awake he made lots of happy noises. At a few weeks old, he began to smile.

Maggie and Bill thought that Benjy, as he was now known, was the most extraordinary baby ever. They never dreamt what was to come.

At around eight months of age,
Benjy began to crawl. It happened at
a weekend, so that his father was not
at work, and both parents were
proudly watching their little son as
he sat, balancing on his nappy-clad
bottom, on the living-room floor.

Then he tipped himself forward on to his hands and knees.

'Oh, Bill!' said Maggie. 'I think he's going to crawl!'

And so he did.

Backwards.

It wasn't a very long crawl. Benjy stopped and sat up on his bottom again, while his parents watched. They expected that next time he would realize his mistake and begin to crawl forwards as all babies do.

Except their baby, it seemed. For Benjy set off again in reverse gear, until his feet touched the wall and he could go no further. He twisted his fat neck far enough round to see what was stopping him, and then he humped himself round to face the wall and away he went again, backwards, smiling happily up at his dumbfounded parents.

'He *is* crawling!' said Maggie. 'We ought to be saying, "*What* a clever boy."'

'We would be,' said Bill, 'if he were crawling forwards.'

'But surely,' said Maggie, 'that makes what he's doing twice as clever? I bet no other baby could do that. Why do you think he's crawling backwards, Bill?'

'I've no idea,' replied Bill. But at that instant he did have an idea, a rather crazy one. Both Maggie and I, he thought, always like travelling with our backs to the engine, going backwards in fact. Could Benjy somehow have inherited this?

'I shouldn't worry your head about it, Maggie,' he said. 'Next time he crawls, it'll be forwards, I'm sure.'

But it wasn't.

Whenever and wherever Benjy Butterworth crawled, it was always backwards.

There comes a time when babies get up off their hands and feet and manage to stand upright. Quite soon after that, they begin to toddle.

Though neither said anything to the other, it occurred to both Maggie and Bill that Benjy might just be different from all other toddlers, who toddle forwards. But

then they each dismissed the thought
from their mind, until the day came
when Benjy took his first steps.

Bill had gone to work and Maggie
was cooking. Benjy was sitting in the
middle of the kitchen floor. Then he
levered himself up with the aid of a
nearby chair and stood upright on
his two fat feet.

'Oh, Benjy!' cried Maggie. '*What* a
clever boy!'

She turned from the stove and
moved close to him and held out her
arms.

'Come to Mummy, darling!' she
cried.

Benjy smiled and moved away
from her, backwards. Because he
couldn't see where he was going, he

very soon fell over, and it was as
Maggie was picking him up that she
had an idea – a rather crazy one.
Both Bill and I, she thought, always
like travelling with our backs to the
engine, going backwards in fact.
Could Benjy somehow have
inherited this?

When her husband arrived home from work she told him that Benjy had taken his first steps.

Bill took a deep breath.

'Forwards?' he asked.

Maggie shook her head.

'Oh, Bill!' she said. 'And he keeps falling down.'

'Because he can't see where he's going?'

'Yes.'

'Well,' said Bill, 'we'll just have to break him of these habits. We'll have to train him, like you would a puppy.'

'With rewards, you mean?' asked Maggie.

'Yes. A biscuit, say. We'll give him a biscuit every time he does it right.'

So Maggie fetched a biscuit, and
Bill waited until Benjy had hoisted
himself to his feet once more. Then
he squatted before his little son and
held out the biscuit and said, 'Come,
Benjy! Good boy! Come to Daddy!'

But Benjy carefully – he was
getting better at balancing – turned
his back on his father and began –
slowly, so as not to fall down – to
toddle backwards towards him, one
fat hand held out behind him for the
biscuit.

Benjy became very good at toddling
backwards. Soon he could go as fast
as a normal baby going forwards,
but he tended to bump into things
and trip over things because he

couldn't see too well where he was going.

Then his father had a good idea.

Bill knew how important rear-view mirrors were to drivers, so he persuaded Maggie to let Benjy hold a mirror of hers that had a handle, just to see what would happen.

At first, Benjy held it up right in front of his face and looked into it and saw himself and smiled and said, 'Benjy!' But then he held the mirror a bit further away and saw the part of the room that was behind him. Now he could toddle much more safely, and his mother

had to buy herself another hand-
mirror, for Benjy wouldn't give up
his new aid to safe reversing.

By now, Maggie and Bill Butterworth
had become accustomed to their son's
method of progress and were not
surprised that it did not alter when
toddling became walking. Benjy, rear-
view mirror always in hand, went
round the house and the garden with
the greatest of ease. Luckily the
Butterworths lived in a bungalow.

'Just think!' said Maggie. 'If we'd
had stairs! What a worry that would
have been!'

But they did have another worry,
which was that Benjy seemed in no
hurry to talk. True, he said the odd
single word like 'Benjy' or 'Daddy' or

'Mummy' or 'potty', but when he reached an age where most children are beginning to speak little sentences, he still hadn't even strung two words together.

One day he did, and his parents received yet another shock.

It happened one breakfast time. Benjy was feeding himself now, after a fashion, and when he'd shoved the last of his breakfast into and on to his face, his mother took his plate away and wiped his mouth and said, 'Good boy.' Benjy smiled at her.

'Boy good,' he said.

Bill and Maggie looked at one another.

Bill cleared his throat, a trifle nervously.

'Good Benjy,' he said.

'Benjy good,' replied his son.

'Bill,' said Maggie in a sort of hoarse whisper, 'you don't think ...?'

'No, no,' said her husband. 'He just got the words in the wrong order, that's all, didn't you, Benjy?

Here, have a bit of this.' And he cut a finger of toast and buttered it and held it out.

Benjy took it.

'Say "Thank you, Daddy",' said Maggie.

'Daddy you thank,' said Benjy.

His mother and father looked at one another again.

Then Maggie muttered, 'He talks backwards.'

Benjy smiled broadly.

'Backwards talks he,' he replied.

That was just the start of it, of course.

As Benjy grew older, he talked more and more. By now the whole family – grandparents, uncles and aunts, cousins – knew about Benjy, though they all kept quiet about him.

But for all of them, particularly, of course, his mother and father, conversation with him was not easy. Understanding what Benjy was saying meant that you had to learn his language. Everything he said had to be turned back to front. For example, he might come into a room – in reverse, rear-view mirror in hand – and say, 'You are how, James Uncle, hello?' Or perhaps something longer, like, 'It wipe you can, running is nose my, Granny.'

Maggie and Bill grew so used to translating his speech that they sometimes fell into the habit themselves.

'School to goes he when,' said Maggie to her husband, 'happen will whatever?'

'Knows Heaven,' Bill replied. 'Oh, goodness me, Maggie, we must stop doing this; we're getting as bad as Benjy.'

'I know,' his wife said. 'It's catching, isn't it?'

And so it was, as they found when Benjy did start school. He walked there on the first day of term, holding his mother's hand (but facing, of course, in the opposite direction from her). When they arrived, Maggie took him into the Reception Class.

'This is Benjy,' she said to the teacher, who wore a look of

astonishment at the sight of a small
boy walking into her classroom
backwards and then holding up a
hand-mirror so that he could see her
over his shoulder.

'Hello, Benjy,' the teacher said.

'My name is Miss Wood. Aren't you going to turn round and look at me then?'

'I'm afraid he won't, said Maggie. 'He's always done everything backwards. In fact, we think he's pretty bright.' And to Benjy she said, 'Say, "Hello, Miss Wood."'

'Wood Miss hello,' said Benjy.

Maggie felt very nervous when she went to collect her son at the end of the school day. Would the other children have laughed at him and mocked his way of walking and talking and made him unhappy?

In fact, he looked perfectly happy and he seemed to have made some friends already. As they left, several small boys and girls called out 'Bye,

Benjy!' and he replied, 'Joe, bye' or, 'Tomorrow you see Polly, bye.'

When Maggie went to collect Benjy the next day, she noticed that several children walked out of the Reception Classroom backwards. In fact, one little boy *ran* backwards until he fell over and began to howl. Then she heard one little girl say to another, 'Time the what's?' to which the reply was 'Three past five.'

At the end of that first week, Maggie had a phone call from the head teacher. Could she and her husband come to the school that evening?

'Shall we say six o'clock?' he asked.

'With Benjy?' said Maggie.

'No!' said the head teacher. 'No, no, I want to talk to you both about Benjy. I expect you can get someone to look after him for half an hour?'

So that Friday evening Bill and Maggie, having parked Benjy with one of his aunts (who could speak Benjytalk well), went to talk to the head teacher.

'Mr and Mrs Butterworth,' he said gloomily – he looked very tired, they noticed – 'I fear that I have unhappy news for you. I know that your little boy has only been attending this school for five days, though it seems much longer, and I also know from his teacher that he is a very bright little boy. His reading, for example, is far in advance of the other children in the

Reception Class, except that, as I'm
sure you know, he reads everything
backwards.

'Indeed this reversal of the
normal ways of speech and
movement is at the root of the
problem that now confronts me,

which is that Benjy's unusual ways have already become a kind of cult among the children in his class. Many of them, Miss Wood tells me, consider his behaviour "cool" and have taken to copying Benjy by also walking and talking backwards. Not only that, the habit is spreading. Several of the other children have begun to adopt these practices, and indeed one boy was seen to run backwards at a football and kick it with his heel.

'As far as Miss Wood is concerned, I think the final straw was when, this morning, she began the day as usual by saying "Good morning" to her class, whereupon *all* of them replied, "Wood Miss morning good. All, morning good." I must therefore tell you, Mr and Mrs Butterworth, that with great regret I have come to the conclusion that I cannot be responsible for your son's education.'

The head teacher paused.

'Go must he,' he said and then he went red in the face.

'Er, what I mean is,' he said, 'he must go.'

Benjy wasn't too happy when his parents told him that he couldn't go to that school any more.

'Not why?' he said.

'It's because of you doing everything backwards,' they said. 'Don't you think you could try to do as everyone else does?'

'Try walking forwards,' Maggie said. 'Now.'

'Go on,' said Bill. 'Have a go.'

'Can't I,' Benjy said.

'What are we going to do, Bill?' said Maggie that evening.

'Try another school, I suppose,' said her husband.

'But the same thing will happen.'

However, the same thing didn't happen, because every school to which they applied said that they were very sorry but they already had a full Reception Class. Miss Wood's head teacher had not been slow to spread the news.

'There's only one thing for it, Maggie,' said Bill.

'What's that?'

'Home education. You'll have to teach Benjy, here at home.'

'Oh, thanks a bunch!' cried Maggie. 'It's hard work teaching anyway, let alone remembering that everything has to be done back to front.'

'Not everything,' Bill said.

'What d'you mean?'

'Well, what about numbers? Three times seven is the same as seven times three. And two plus eight makes ten just as eight plus two does.'

'Oh yes, and I suppose that twenty divided by four is the same as four divided by twenty!' said Maggie. 'Home education indeed! I can tell you exactly what will happen. At the

end of it you won't just have a son
who does everything in reverse,
you'll have a wife doing it too.'

'Perhaps,' said Bill, 'we ought first
of all to take him to see a doctor.'

So they did, and Benjy (of course)

walked backwards into the consulting room, his rear-view mirror at the ready.

When the doctor asked him his name, he replied (as you might expect), 'Butterworth Benjy.' Then the doctor asked Benjy a number of questions, and each time Benjy gave his answer in reverse. If it was a long answer, either Maggie or Bill would translate for the doctor's benefit.

'I must confess, Mr and Mrs Butterworth,' he said finally, 'that I have never in my long experience come across a case like this. Tell me, has Benjy always behaved this way?'

'Oh yes,' they said.

'It occurs to me,' the doctor went on, 'that there is a possibility that this condition could be genetic. But then I don't suppose that either of you ever behaved in such a way?'

'Oh no,' they said.

Each shot a glance at the other and at that instant each remembered the idea – the rather crazy idea – that had occurred to each of them when Benjy was very small. Both of us, thought Bill and Maggie once again, always like travelling with our backs to the engine, going backwards in fact. Could Benjy somehow have inherited this?

'Ah well, try not to worry!' said the doctor in a jolly voice. 'One thing is certain, Benjy is in very good health. We must just hope that his little problem corrects itself as he gets older. When it comes to riding a bike, for example – very difficult to do backwards, ha ha! And of course later on, when he's old enough to drive, well, I hardly think that he'll be whizzing up the motorway at seventy miles per hour in reverse, ha

ha ha! We must just wait and see.'

'You think he'll grow out of it, do you, doctor?' asked Maggie.

'Children do grow out of things,' said the doctor cheerily, 'so I expect you will, Benjy, won't you?'

'Know don't I,' said Benjy.

The next time Bill went up to town on the 8.23, the train was packed. The only seat he could find was one facing the engine. As he sat there, looking out of the window and seeing things rushing towards him instead of rushing away from him, he realized how crazy it was to imagine that Benjy could have inherited his parents' preference for travelling backwards.

'You won't believe it,' he said to Maggie that evening, 'but I've had this idea …' And he told her about it.

'I've had exactly the same idea,' said Maggie, 'but it's crazy, isn't it, Bill?'

'Yes, it is. Whatever is wrong with Benjy is nothing to do with us. It's something that goes on inside his head.'

'In his brain, you're saying?'

'Yes. The more I think about it, the more sure I am that he must have been born with some sort of loose electrical connection in his brain, some bit of it that's the wrong way round.'

'Back to front, you mean?'

36

'Yes. Though of course he doesn't do everything back to front. He sits up at table the right way, and in the car too, and in front of the telly, and he'd probably have sat quite happily in the seat I had on the train this morning.'

'But what can we do?' said Maggie.

'I honestly don't know. Perhaps he'll grow out of it, as the doctor said. In the meantime, no school will have him, so –'

'Yes, yes, all right,' Maggie interrupted. 'I'll teach him at home, the best I can. We can use the school programmes on TV. I'll manage somehow.'

'I'm sure you will,' said Bill. 'If

only you could teach him the right
way to walk and talk. How I'd love
to come home from work one day
and find our Benjy behaving like a
normal little boy!'

'What a shock that would give
you!' Maggie said.

She remembered these words
some weeks later.

The home education wasn't going too badly. Benjy seemed to pick things up pretty quickly, and Maggie had managed to train herself not to fall into Benjytalk. But it was tiring work for her, so each afternoon she and Benjy would go for a walk to have a break and get some fresh air. Benjy walked backwards of course, one hand holding his mother's, the other his rear-view mirror.

They were not very long, these walks, for Benjy's method of progress was more tiring for him than the normal way of walking, and there would come a point where he would say, 'Mum, please home go we can?'

But one day they had walked a little further than usual when Maggie noticed that the sky was becoming threateningly dark. A storm was brewing, it was soon plain, and they were in for a soaking if they didn't hurry home. Big drops of rain began to fall and suddenly there was a rumble of thunder.

'Quickly, Benjy!' his mother said, half dragging him along as they made for a gate that led from the fields into the garden of the Butterworths' bungalow.

'Faster go can't I,' panted Benjy, and at that instant there was a great clap of thunder right above their heads. Maggie heard a sizzling sound and saw a blazingly bright light. Then there came a great cracking tearing noise as the lightning struck a nearby tree. There was so much noise that she didn't hear a little tinkling sound like breaking glass.

'Come on, Benjy, come on!' she cried, taking a fresh grip on his hand, and they ran together through the gate and into their garden.

It was not until they were halfway up the garden path that Maggie saw to her amazement that Benjy was running forwards. Into the bungalow they dashed, while outside the rain poured down, the thunder clapped, the lightning flashed.

'Benjy!' gasped Maggie. 'You were running … forwards!'

'I was, wasn't I?' said Benjy.

Maggie, translating automatically as usual, thought he was saying, 'I wasn't, was I?'

'You were! You were!' she cried.

Benjy smiled.

'I know, Mum,' he said. 'I must say, it's much easier running that way.'

He held up the hand-mirror. The glass in it, Maggie could see, was splintered.

'I shan't need this thing any more,' Benjy said.

'But you're talking forwards too,' said Maggie in a kind of hoarse whisper. She picked up a book and shoved it at him.

'Read that first line,' she said, and he read it, from the left end to the right end, just as we all do.

Maggie hugged him.

'Oh, Benjy!' she cried. 'Whatever's happened?'

'It must have been the lightning,' Benjy said.

'But you're not hurt, not burned, you're not in pain, are you?'

'No,' said Benjy. 'But when that lightning flash came, I felt a shock inside my head, a sort of electric shock, and suddenly everything seemed different.'

'Just wait till your father gets home!' Maggie said. 'He's going to get a shock all right!'

'Hello, you two,' said Bill Butterworth when he arrived home from work. 'Had a good day, have you?'

'We certainly have,' said his wife, grinning from ear to ear.

'What's up with you, Maggie?' said Bill. 'You look like the cat that's eaten the cream.'

'We've got a bit of a surprise for you,' said Maggie. 'Haven't we, Benjy?'

'Yes,' said Benjy.

'Well?' asked Bill. Nothing surprising about Benjy saying 'Yes', he thought. He always just says 'Yes' or 'No', single words like those; it's sentences he says backwards.

'Show Daddy, Benjy,' said Maggie.

So Benjy walked, forwards, towards his father and held out to him a sheet of paper. On it he had written in large letters

DAD EVENING GOOD

(and after the words he'd put a cross)
and below that he'd written

GOOD EVENING DAD

(and after that, a tick).

'Oh, Benjy!' said his father. 'And you walked forwards to me! Didn't you? Say something to me, Benjy – anything!'

'Well, you see, Dad,' said Benjy, 'Mum and I went for a walk and we got caught in a thunderstorm and there was a big flash of lightning and I got a sort of shock inside my head and now everything's happening the right way round. I can read right and talk right and walk right and run right. It's cool, Dad, don't you think?'

'It must have been just as I thought,' said Bill to Maggie that night. 'I said so, didn't I? He had some sort of loose connection in his brain and the electrical discharge from the bolt of lightning put it right.'

'How clever you are,' said Maggie. She sighed happily.

'No more home education,' she said.

'What d'you mean?'

'Why, any school will take Benjy now. There's no way that anyone could possibly say that Benjy Butterworth was back to front.'

The Hitmus-Potmus

Bartholomew Bean was a very
rude boy. His favourite word was
'Shan't'.

When his mother, Mrs Bean, told
him to wash his hands or clean his
teeth or wipe his shoes,
Bartholomew said, 'Shan't.'

When his father, Mr Bean, told him

to mind his manners, Bartholomew
said, 'Shan't.'

One day, Mr Bean's brother, who
had lived in Africa for many years,
came to stay the night. He was very
tall and thin, and everybody called
him Runner Bean.

'Say hello to your Uncle Runner,'
said Mrs Bean to Bartholomew.

'Shan't,' said Bartholomew.

'Do as your mother says,' said Mr
Bean.

'Shan't,' said Bartholomew.

'Good job you don't live in
Mopotobutu,' said Uncle Runner.

'Why?' asked Bartholomew.

'In Mopotobutu,' said Uncle Runner, 'boys who are rude get eaten by the Hitmus-Potmus.'

'Hitmus-Potmus!' said Bartholomew. 'You mean hippopotamus, and they eat grass, not people. You're stupid, you are.'

'Bartholomew!' cried Mr and Mrs Bean. 'Say you're sorry to Uncle Runner.'

'Shan't,' said Bartholomew.

'In Mopotobutu,' said Uncle Runner, 'when the Hitmus-Potmus hears of a rude boy, it comes up from the murky depths of the Eezipeezi River and swallows him whole, at one gulp.'

'Rubbish!' said Bartholomew.

'Bartholomew!' cried Mr and Mrs
Bean. 'Go straight to bed!'

'Shan't,' said Bartholomew.

'Bartholomew,' said Uncle Runner,
'I'm not here for long, so I hope
you'll stay downstairs and talk to me.'

'Shan't,' said Bartholomew, and he
stumped off up to his bedroom.

'You and your Hitmus-Potmus,
Runner!' said Mr Bean.

Runner Bean laughed.

'It's a well-known story in
Mopotobutu,' he said, 'specially near
the Eezipeezi River.'

'You'll give the boy nightmares,'
said Mrs Bean.

'Shall I?' said Runner Bean.
'Perhaps I'd better go up and see
him.'

But when he looked into Bartholomew's bedroom and said, 'Sleep well', Bartholomew only answered, 'Shan't.'

'You are a very rude boy,' said Uncle Runner.

'And you are a silly old fool,' said Bartholomew.

'OK,' said Uncle Runner. 'If that's the way you want it.'

Much later that night, when the other Beans were fast asleep, Uncle Runner sat on the bed in the spare room, holding a photo of Bartholomew. As he stared at it, he chanted (in Mopotobutunese):

'Hitmus-Potmus, mumbo-jumbo.
Hitmus-Potmus, gully-gully-gumbo.

Hitmus-Potmus in your dream
Makes you scream and scream and
scream.'

And at that very moment Bartholomew
woke up, yelling his head off.

'Save me!' he cried as his mother
and father came rushing in. 'It's the
Hitmus-Potmus! It came into my
room and it said, "You are a very
rude boy" and it opened its great jaws
wide and it was going to swallow me
whole, in one gulp! Oh Mummy,
Daddy, I'll never ever be rude again!'

Next morning, when Runner Bean
was leaving, Mr Bean called to
Bartholomew, 'Come quickly.' And
Bartholomew came quickly.

'Shake hands nicely with your

uncle,' said Mrs Bean, and
Bartholomew shook hands nicely.

'Say goodbye,' they said, and
Bartholomew said, 'Goodbye, Uncle
Runner.'

'Goodbye, Bartholomew,' said
Uncle Runner. 'You must come and
stay with me one day.'

'In Mopotobutu?' said
Bartholomew.

'Yes.'

'By the Eezipeezi River?'

'Yes.'

Bartholomew Bean looked up at his
tall thin uncle.

'You're asking me to come and stay
in the land of the Hitmus-Potmus?' he
said.

'Yes.'

'Well, I hope you'll excuse me, Uncle Runner,' said Bartholomew very politely, 'but there's only one answer to that.'

'What?' said Uncle Runner.

Bartholomew smiled.

'Shan't,' he said.

Brown's Bones

A long time ago there lived, in the middle of the Midlands, an unusual wizard by the name of Brown. Actually his other names were Reginald (after his father) Cedric Algernon, but, liking none of these, he preferred to be called simply Brown.

He was unusual because he didn't look a bit like a wizard. He didn't wear strange clothes or funny hats, and he was young. What's more, he was a rather nice-looking boy, so that a lot of girls fancied him rotten.

They didn't know he was a wizard, of course. They didn't know that he

could perform the most amazing
trick that wizards ever did.

He could turn people into animals.

Brown didn't know either until,
when he was in his teens, he found
out quite by chance.

It all began when Brown found the
skeleton of a small bird in the

garden. He gathered up the little bones that had been picked clean by the ants, and took them into the living room. His father, Reginald Brown, was sitting there reading the paper and drinking a glass of beer. Brown did not get on too well with his father, who was a rude and grumpy man.

'Dad,' said Brown, 'what sort of bird d'you suppose this was?' And he showed his father the bones.

'How do I know, you stupid boy?' said Reginald Brown without even looking at them.

Brown was hurt. He never speaks to me nicely, he told himself, and anyway he's the stupid one. And he took himself off to his bedroom.

Moodily, he began to smash up the little bones with the hammer from his toy carpentry set. With a pair of pliers he broke them into even smaller pieces, and then, using a sheet of sandpaper, he reduced some of them to a fine powder.

Carefully, Brown put the bone-dust into a little box. A wicked thought had entered his head. I'll put this in his rotten old beer, he said to himself.

Back downstairs, he hung about until his father got up to poke the fire, and then he tipped the bone-dust into Reginald Brown's glass and waited. See how he likes that! thought Brown. But he was not prepared for what happened next.

One minute his father raised the glass and took a drink.

The next, he had disappeared, while the glass fell on the floor and smashed.

On the seat of his armchair was a sparrow, which gave an angry-sounding chirrup before flying out of the open window. Brown's mother came in.

'Where's your dad?' she said.

'Gone out,' said Brown.

Mrs Brown looked at the broken glass and the spilled beer.

'He must have been in a hurry,' she said.

'He was,' said Brown. 'He fairly flew.'

Brown's next step was to repeat

the experiment with different sorts of bone. That night they had lamb chops for supper, and the next day the Vicar called.

Brown had never much liked the Vicar, who always addressed him as 'Cedric', but he was quick enough to offer to fill up his teacup while Mrs Brown was fetching some biscuits.

She came back just too late to see a big lamb run out of the house and off down the road, bleating loudly.

'Where's the Vicar?' she said.

'Gone out,' said Brown.

'He hadn't finished his second cup,' said Mrs Brown.

'He'd had enough,' said Brown.

Next day it was roast chicken, and Brown, working away on a

drumstick with his toy carpentry set,
wondered who'd be next. Not Mum,
he thought; she's not as bad as Dad
was, and anyway I still need
someone to do the cooking and the
washing and all that.

The problem was solved when his
Auntie Barbara, Reginald Brown's
sister, dropped in the following
Sunday just before lunch. Auntie
Barbara always dropped in just
before Sunday lunch. Her brother
kept a bottle of her favourite sweet
sherry specially for her.

'Where's Reginald?' said Auntie
Barbara.

'Don't know,' said Mrs Brown. 'He
went out in a hurry, Tuesday I think
it was, and he's never come back.'

'Funny,' said Auntie Barbara. 'The Vicar's disappeared too. The curate took the service this morning.'

Brown had never much liked his Auntie Barbara, who always called him 'Algie', and he hurried to fetch her a second glass of sherry while his mother was seeing to the lunch.

She came back just too late to see
a large white hen scamper out
through the French windows and
across the lawn.

'Where's Auntie Barbara?' she
said.

'Done a runner,' said Brown.

'Why? She didn't even finish her
second sherry.'

'I think it upset her,' said Brown.

'And how did this get here?' said
his mother, for on the seat of Auntie
Barbara's chair was a new-laid egg.

Over the next few years it was
remarkable how many people in the
middle of the Midlands disappeared.

At the same time, there were
continual reports – especially around

the area where the Browns lived – of stray animals found wandering the streets. As well as chickens and lambs, there were pigs, and little calves, and large bullocks, and ducks, and once, just after Christmas, a turkey.

The police were baffled and, every now and then, the newspapers would run stories with headlines such as

MYSTERY IN MIDLANDS MULTIPLIES.

Brown, meantime, had grown up into a handsome young man and the girls fancied him even more.

Some of them had cause to regret this, for the wizard was very particular and soon tired of those who talked too much or too little, or didn't laugh at his jokes, or chose expensive things to eat when he took them out.

So the numbers of stray animals in the Midlands grew even more, till one day Brown fell head over heels in love with a girl with red hair and brown eyes and quick wits and a black cat. Unfortunately, she didn't seem all that interested in Brown, and when he asked her to marry him, she said, 'No, thanks.'

'Why not?' said Brown.

'Because you're a nice-looking boy, but ordinary. I shall only marry someone who is different from everyone else.'

'But I am different!' cried Brown. 'I am a wizard!'

'Pull the other one,' said the redhead.

'I'll show you,' said Brown, and he took her into what had been Reginald Brown's study. Here he now kept his toy carpentry set, and there were shelves holding rows of little boxes, labelled CHICKEN, CALF, LAMB and so on, each box filled with bone-dust.

Brown took down a box marked PIG.

'If I was to pour some of this into a drink – a glass of wine, say – and you were to drink it, you'd turn into a pig. I tell you, I'm a wizard.'

'I don't believe a word of it,' said the redhead. And at that moment

Mrs Brown called, 'I've made coffee if you two would like some.'

So desperate was Brown to prove his powers to his beloved that he said to his mother, 'I think I heard a knock at the front door.' And then, making sure the girl was watching, he laced his mother's cup with pig bone-dust.

'Nobody there,' she said when she came back, and she sat down and took a swig of coffee and turned into a big fat sow.

'Brown,' said the redhead, as together they drove the loudly grunting animal out through the front door, 'I owe you an apology. You *are* a wizard.'

You horrible, horrible man, she thought.

'Well then,' said Brown, 'will you marry me?'

'On one condition.'

'What's that?'

'I've had almost enough of my mother. But I don't fancy her as a pig. Something smaller, I think. Can you fix that?'

'A duck?' said Brown. 'We had duck last week. I've got some nice fresh duck bone-dust.'

'No,' said the redhead. 'A mouse, I think.'

'Right!' said Brown. 'We've plenty of mice about the place. I'll set a trap tonight.'

'When will you have everything ready?'

'Oh, tomorrow, if I can catch one.'

Brown did catch a mouse that night, and next day he went round to the redhead's house with a little box of mouse bone-dust.

He found his loved one alone, except for her black cat.

'Where's your mother?' said Brown.

'Gone out. She'll be back soon. Like a cup of tea?'

'Yes, please.'

So the redhead made a pot of tea and poured three cups: one for herself, one for Brown, and one for her mother.

'Won't your mother's tea get cold?' said Brown.

'No, she'll be back any minute. Put the powder in her cup, Brown,

there's a good wizard, and then have
a look out of the window and see if
she's coming up the road.'

So Brown poured in the mouse
bone-dust, and while he was looking
out of the window, the redhead

swapped that cup with the one she'd given him before.

And Reginald Cedric Algernon Brown, son of the late Mr and Mrs Brown, drank his tea and turned into a mouse.

'He's all yours, puss,' said the redhead to her black cat.

Little Liar

Lionel went to tea with his Auntie Marigold.

'Now then, Lionel,' said Auntie Marigold, 'what do we do before we have our tea?'

'We wash our hands, Auntie,' said Lionel.

'That's right,' said his aunt. 'You

always do that at home, I'm sure.'

'Oh yes, Auntie,' said Lionel, and
he went to the bathroom and turned

on the taps, full, to make a noise, just
as he did at home. Then he turned
them off again.

'Did you wash them properly,
Lionel?' said his aunt when he came
back.

'Oh yes, Auntie,' said Lionel.

Lionel was a little liar.

'Now,' said Auntie Marigold when
they were sitting at the tea-table,
'here is a glass of milk for you,
Lionel.' She poured him some milk
and poured herself a cup of tea.

'And what would you like to eat?'
she said.

'Cake, please,' said Lionel.

'Now, now,' said Auntie Marigold.
'You know the rules, Lionel. What

do we always have first, before we have our cake?'

'Plain bread and butter,' said Lionel.

'Take a piece then.'

Lionel took a piece.

'That's right,' said Auntie Marigold. 'Nice fresh milk and a nice piece of plain bread and butter. You like both those things, don't you?'

'Oh yes, Auntie,' said Lionel.

Lionel was a little liar.

'Oh look, Auntie,' he said. 'That's a pretty picture.'

'Which picture?' said Auntie Marigold.

'The one on the wall behind you,' said Lionel, and when his aunt turned round to look, he poured the milk into a nearby pot plant and slipped the bread and butter under the table, where Auntie Marigold's Pekinese was waiting.

'Yes,' said his aunt, turning back again, 'it is a nice picture. Goodness me, you haven't drunk your milk and eaten your bread and butter already, have you?'

'Oh yes, Auntie,' said Lionel.

Lionel was a little liar.

'Right then. Now you can have your cake and eat it. Would you like a nice slice?'

'Oh yes, please, Auntie.'

'As big as this?'

'Bigger.'

'As this?'

'Bigger still.'

'Lionel,' said Auntie Marigold, 'I trust you are not becoming a greedy boy?'

'Oh no, Auntie,' said Lionel.

Lionel was a little liar.

*

He ate the big slice of cake very
quickly, and when his aunt asked
him what he would like to eat next,
he said, 'More.'

'More what?' said Auntie
Marigold, meaning that Lionel
should have said, 'More, please.'

'More cake,' said Lionel.

'Now, now,' said Auntie Marigold. 'I'm sure your mother never gives you two slices of cake at home.'

'No,' said Lionel, 'she doesn't. She gives me four.'

Lionel was a little liar.

'Oh,' said his aunt. 'Oh very well. I suppose you are a growing boy.' And she cut him another slice.

After the cake, Lionel worked his way through sugar buns and jam doughnuts and brandy snaps and cream slices, until there was nothing left on the tea-table but a plate of chocolate fingers.

'Lionel,' said Auntie Marigold, 'I think you have really had enough.'

'Oh, Auntie,' said Lionel, 'can't I

have some chocolate fingers? I was saving them up till last.'

'Just one,' said his aunt.

'Two?' said Lionel.

'Oh very well,' said Auntie Marigold.

She stood up.

'I must fetch some more hot water for the teapot,' she said.

She looked back as she was leaving the room.

'Only two, mind,' she said. 'Promise?'

'I promise,' said Lionel.

Lionel was a little liar.

The moment his aunt had disappeared from sight, he shoved a handful of chocolate fingers into his mouth and chewed and swallowed as fast as he could. He just had time for a second handful before his aunt came back.

She looked at the plate of chocolate fingers.

'Lionel!' she said. 'Do you expect me to believe that you have only had two?'

'Oh yesh, Armpy,' said Lionel with his mouth full.

'Lionel!' said his aunt again. 'I trust you are not becoming a little liar?'

Lionel swallowed.

'Oh no, Auntie,' he said.

He swallowed again.

Then he began to turn a sort of pale greenish colour.

Then he put one hand on his stomach and the other to his throat.

'Lionel!' cried Auntie Marigold. 'I trust you are not going to be sick!'

'Oh no, Auntie,' said Lionel in a feeble voice.

But Lionel was a little liar.